Digging for
BURIED TREASURE

by Lisa Thompson
illustrated by Brenda Cantell

™
sundance
A Haights Cross Communications ✈ Company

A Haights Cross Communications Company

Published by Sundance Publishing
One Beeman Road
P.O. Box 740
Northborough, MA 01532-0740
800-343-8204
www.sundancepub.com

First published as Treasure Trackers by
Blake Education, Locked Bag 2022, Glebe 2037, Australia
Exclusive United States Distribution: Sundance Publishing

ISBN 0-7608-9330-6

Contents

CANADA

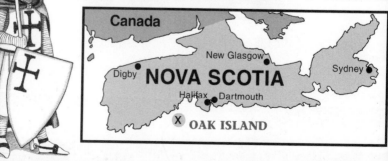

OAK ISLAND

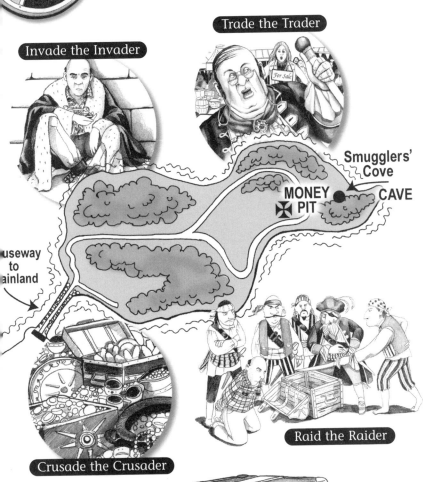

Trade the Trader

Invade the Invader

Smugglers'
Cove

MONEY
✠ PIT

CAVE

Causeway
to
Mainland

Raid the Raider

Crusade the Crusader

Chapter 1

The Unwelcome Sign

The signs that blocked the deserted causeway to Oak Island were very clear.

WARNING
Do NOT Enter!
Keep Out!
NO Trespassers!
24-Hour Security Surveillance and Dog Patrol

Ricky stepped out of the car and followed his best friend Mia and her Uncle Earl. They stopped at a high mesh fence that didn't move in the strong wind. The gate was heavily padlocked.

Mrs. Oxley, the woman who had driven them, stayed by the car. Three days earlier, Mrs. Oxley's cat, Curiosity, had dug up a strange object on the mainland beach that faced Oak Island. Mrs. Oxley had sent it to Uncle Earl. She had never imagined, however, that Curiosity's discovery would cause such excitement.

Because of his worldwide reputation as the expert's expert in the field of archaeology, Uncle Earl was often presented with strange things. People hoped that he would identify them as valuable lost treasure. Most of the time, they were nothing special. But the double-headed coin sent by Mrs. Oxley had intrigued him.

"Incredible! Unbelievable!" Uncle Earl had exclaimed.

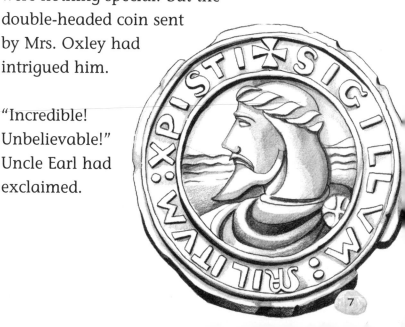

Uncle Earl believed that the coin could hold the clue to finding an immense treasure. It was the treasure at the center of the world's longest and most costly treasure hunt—the Oak Island Money Pit!

"See," said Mrs. Oxley, "it's just as I said. No one lives on the island anymore, except Bill Campbell, and he doesn't like visitors. He's lived alone, guarding the Pit since they stopped digging more than two years ago. He won't let anyone in, and he won't leave the island. People think that hunting for that treasure has made him weird. Everyone calls him Crazy Campbell." As she said his name, the hairs on Curiosity's coat shot straight up. Mrs. Oxley stroked her. "Calm down, Curiosity. Crazy Campbell's not going to hurt you."

Uncle Earl checked the lock on the gate. It was very rusty but still held firm. "It looks like no one's been through here for a long time."

Thud! The wind banged one of the signs against the fence. "This place is creepy," said Mia, pulling her jacket tightly around her. "What kind of treasure is in this Money Pit?"

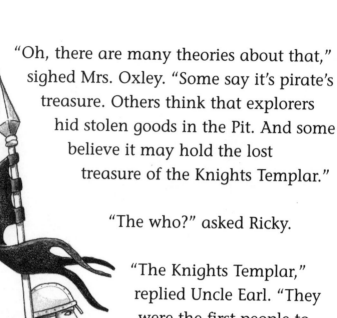

"Oh, there are many theories about that," sighed Mrs. Oxley. "Some say it's pirate's treasure. Others think that explorers hid stolen goods in the Pit. And some believe it may hold the lost treasure of the Knights Templar."

"The who?" asked Ricky.

"The Knights Templar," replied Uncle Earl. "They were the first people to establish banks. Kings, rulers, and the very wealthy would deposit money with the Templars in one place and withdraw it somewhere else."

Mrs. Oxley nodded. "The Knights became wealthy and powerful. They were a secret society. People have been trying to find the Knights' treasure in the Money Pit for hundreds of years. But there is a system of traps and doors in the Pit that no one can outwit. It is so clever that it certainly points to the Knights Templar. Each time someone thinks that they are about to discover the treasure, the Pit's shaft floods with water."

Mia and Ricky walked along the fence to get a better view of Oak Island. When they returned to the car, they found Uncle Earl in the front seat, sending e-mails on his laptop. "There," he said, sending his last message. "I've contacted everyone who might be able to help us, including Mr. Campbell. Hopefully we'll be able to meet with him soon."

Mrs. Oxley stared at Uncle Earl. "Earl, I'm not setting foot on that island. If you want to go, you can go on your own."

"But . . ." Uncle Earl started. Mrs. Oxley held up her hand to stop him.

"Look, I'm happy to help you, but I don't want to deal with the curse."

"You don't really believe in that, do you?" asked Uncle Earl.

"What curse?" Ricky and Mia asked together.

"The Money Pit curse, of course," Mrs. Oxley replied. "It goes:

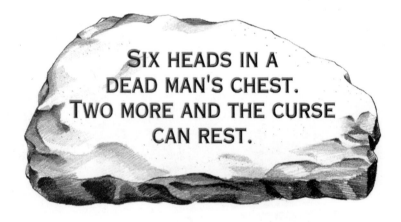

SIX HEADS IN A
DEAD MAN'S CHEST.
TWO MORE AND THE CURSE
CAN REST.

It was written on a piece of stone that was found when they pulled the last dead man out of the Pit. After that, everyone stopped looking for the treasure. Everyone, that is, except Crazy Campbell. I sure don't want to be the one who puts that curse to rest. I don't care how big the treasure is!"

Ricky and Mia didn't know what to say. The whole thing was getting stranger by the minute. Mrs. Oxley stroked Curiosity. "Now who wants some dinner? I don't know about you, but I'm starving!" she said as she got back into the car.

The group was quiet as they drove away from the locked gate.

CHAPTER 2

Operation Undercover

Mrs. Oxley's house was perched high on a cliff top overlooking Oak Island. The house was full of peculiar things that Mrs. Oxley had collected over the years. "Oh, I'm a real hoarder," she laughed, seeing their surprise. "It's a treasure trove in here."

The walls of her house were lined with framed newspaper clippings and photos of Oak Island, as well as a large, detailed map. Ricky looked out the window to the island and then back at the map. The side of the island that faced them was part of Smugglers' Cove.

Uncle Earl, Ricky, and Mia studied one poster very carefully. It was a cross section of the shaft known as the Money Pit. The poster showed the points where the shaft had flooded with water.

"Whoever made the Pit went to a lot of trouble," said Uncle Earl. "Barricades of oak logs have been found every nine feet. And there's a stone inscribed with the words:

*40 feet below,
1 million pieces of gold."*

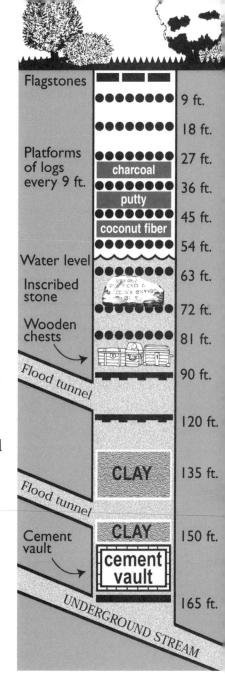

Flagstones

9 ft.

18 ft.

Platforms of logs every 9 ft. 27 ft.

charcoal

36 ft.

putty

45 ft.

coconut fiber

54 ft.

Water level

Inscribed stone 63 ft.

72 ft.

Wooden chests 81 ft.

Flood tunnel 90 ft.

120 ft.

CLAY 135 ft.

Flood tunnel

CLAY 150 ft.

Cement vault

cement vault

165 ft.

UNDERGROUND STREAM

"Just after they found the stone, the shaft filled with water," said Mrs. Oxley.

They talked for hours about the Pit. Each of them had their own ideas about why the Pit was there and what lay at its bottom.

Late that night, Ricky stared across at the island. He wondered if, like him, Crazy Campbell was awake and thinking about the Pit. Maybe Campbell had already read the e-mail from Uncle Earl. What really was hidden in the Money Pit? Ricky's mind was working overtime as he got into bed.

CRASH! Mia woke with a start and flicked on her bedside lamp. There was Ricky on his hands and knees, searching for the flashlight he had just knocked onto the floor.

"Ricky, what are you doing in my room?" she muttered, as she checked her watch. "It's one o'clock in the morning."

"I need to borrow your flashlight so I can check out Oak Island tonight!" said Ricky.

"What about Crazy Campbell?" gasped Mia. "Can't you wait to see if he'll meet with us?"

Ricky looked at Mia. "That's if he's still on the island."

"What? Ricky, I don't think . . ."

"Look, Mia, no one has actually seen him in a long time. Maybe he was unlucky, and the curse got him, too. If word gets out that he's gone, every man and his dog is going to start looking for the treasure. Even if he is still there, I don't think he's going to let us snoop around. Chances are he's going to make extra sure no one comes near the Pit. The only way to get a look is to go there tonight!"

After finding the flashlight, Ricky stood up. Turning, he said, "Come on, Mia! Are you in? We can take Mrs. Oxley's rowboat across the bay to Smugglers' Cove. Don't you want to see Oak Island and find out what the mystery is really all about?"

Mia hesitated for a moment. Then she whispered, "Of course I do."

She still didn't like the idea of creeping onto the island in the dead of night. What if they ran into Crazy Campbell or one of his security dogs? Not to mention the curse!

CHAPTER 3

The Cave's Secret

They pulled up the rowboat at the southern end of Smugglers' Cove and hid it under some bushes. A full moon lit the beach. There wasn't a sound on the island except for the water lapping the shore.

"Dead quiet, isn't it?" said Ricky.

"Did you have to put it that way?" Mia whispered, looking around.

Suddenly there was a noise at the front of the boat. Mia saw a dark shape balancing on an oar. "Curiosity!" she exclaimed.

Ricky felt his heart begin to beat again. "Crazy cat scared the daylights out of me."

"We'd better grab her and somehow keep her in the boat until we get back. Mrs. Oxley would never forgive us if something happened to her." Mia searched for something to tie her with.

"Yeah," laughed Ricky. "Remember—*curiosity killed the cat!*"

"Shh!" hushed Mia. "Did you hear that noise, Ricky?" She turned and froze. Three growling, black dogs were heading straight for them. Even at a distance, their large, white teeth were visible.

"RUN!" yelled Ricky. "Mia! RUUUNNNN!"

Curiosity sprang from the boat and headed into the trees with Ricky and Mia right behind her. The dogs were in hot pursuit.

"In here," cried Ricky, seeing Curiosity disappear into a cave. Inside, Ricky spotted a boulder near the entrance. "Mia, help me roll this rock," he yelled. "We'll block the hole." Pushing hard, they managed to cover the entrance. They could hear the dogs barking and scratching on the other side.

Ricky and Mia stood there panting. They were completely in the dark.

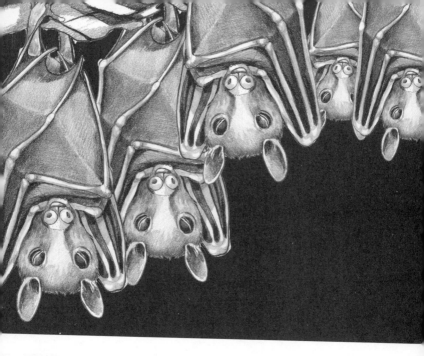

"That sure was close," said Ricky. "Good going,
Mia. I've never seen you run so fast!" He patted
the rock. "This ought to keep them out."

Mia lifted her foot and heard a squishing noise.
The floor of the cave was soft and slimy. "Let's
get some light in this place," she said, turning
on the flashlight. She saw that her feet had
nearly disappeared in a layer of mud.

Ricky looked up to the roof of the cave. "Mia,
we're not alone in here. Don't scream . . . the
last thing we want to do is wake them."

Mia slowly raised her head. The roof of the cave was covered with hundreds and hundreds of bats hanging upside down. Their black wings cloaked their bodies. Ricky heard Mia's sharp intake of breath.

"I just felt something brush my leg," Ricky whispered hoarsely.

Mia shakily directed the flashlight at Ricky's legs. Two amber eyes blinked back.

"Curiosity!" Mia smiled, as Ricky slumped against the cave wall. Curiosity pawed playfully at Ricky before jumping onto a rock ledge.

"It's all right for you!" he said to Curiosity. "You've got nine lives. You can afford to be scared to death a few times."

"Where is she going now?" asked Mia, following the cat. Curiosity stopped in front of a painting on the side of the cave. She meowed softly.

Ricky and Mia moved closer to the painting. It looked very old. Some of the image had been worn away by water trickling down the wall. "It looks like a map of this cave," said Ricky. "Hold the flashlight closer, Mia, so we can get a better look."

The map showed a tunnel at the back of the cave. The beginning of the tunnel was marked with an X. The end was marked with another X and a picture of a shovel and a chest. Next to the map were the instructions:

20 paces down to white rock
12 paces to the right

Mia shined her light toward the back of the cave. "There's a tunnel back there," she said. "I guess if we want to find out more, we'll just have to go into it. Right?"

"Ummm . . . right," was Ricky's nervous reply. "I'll follow you."

"What?" yelped Mia.

"Well, you're the one with the flashlight!" exclaimed Ricky.

"We'll go together," said Mia, holding out her hand. Together they edged toward the tunnel, trying not to wake the bats. Curiosity ran ahead into the darkness.

"I'm glad to see one of us is in a hurry," joked Ricky nervously.

CHAPTER 4

The Treasure Game

Once in the tunnel, they counted 20 paces and found themselves looking at a white rock. From the white rock they turned right and carefully counted 12 paces.

"I guess we just dig," said Mia, "though the instructions didn't say how far down, did they?"

They found two flat, large stones to use as spades. Mia set the flashlight on a ledge. They knelt and started digging. Curiosity stalked around watching them. It was hard work, but just as they were tiring, Ricky's stone struck something hard. They put down their rocks and moved the rest of the dirt with their hands.

"It's a shovel," said a disappointed Ricky.

"That's good," encouraged Mia. "That's what was next to the treasure on the map. We can't be too far away from the chest now."

They took turns using the shovel to heave dirt out of the hole. It seemed ages before they heard another dull thud. This time it was a chest!

"Pay dirt!" Ricky laughed.

"Just like the map showed," cried Mia excitedly.

They lifted the chest out of the hole.

"It's not very big," said Mia, wiping away the dirt to reveal a lock.

"Stand back," said Ricky. He hit the lock a couple of times with the shovel. The lock snapped open.

"Way to go, Ricky!" exclaimed Mia. Curiosity sniffed the chest. Mia and Ricky each grabbed a side of the lid. "On the count of three," said Mia. "Ready, one . . . two . . . three!"

They flung open the lid.

They stared speechlessly at each other. Finally Ricky asked, "What do you think it is, Mia? It doesn't look like much of a treasure to me."

Mia put her hand into the chest and pulled out a flat disk with a spinning arrow attached to its center. The disk was divided into four sections, each a different color. On the disk, the words *Fortune's wheel* were engraved. The words *Fortune's arrow* were engraved on the arrow.

Ricky looked inside the chest and pulled out a crumbling piece of paper. He read the words on it aloud:

Behold Fortune's Wheel and Arrow.

Fortune has a part to play
In what we do from day to day.
Some days are rich and others meager.
To stay on top, you must be eager.

So if you want to find your treasure,
Work out how to fortune measure.

Spin the arrow and make a note of what you be.
For the treasure will change with each assignee.

Yellow: Trade the Trader
Red: Invade the Invader
Blue: Crusade the Crusader
Green: Raid the Raider

Be quick at the task or fortune fades.
Look out for me on each escapade.
Miss me once, and the treasure is lost.
Only then will you know the true cost.

Spin away and start to play.

"What kind of game is this?" cried Mia. They read the words once more, trying to make sense of the riddle.

"I guess we'll get it when we start to play," said Ricky, giving the arrow a spin. It landed on Yellow. "That's Trade . . ."

Everything was spinning. Screaming, Mia and Ricky tumbled through space.

CHAPTER 5

Trading with the Trader

"Well, that's just not my problem," the auctioneer hissed nastily to Mia. "A deal is a deal, and you signed the contract. That means that you agreed to pay the cost of your passage by working as an indentured servant. So look happy! I want a good bid for your contract."

Ricky looked around and tried to figure out where he was. It seemed to be a crowded marketplace. Nodding toward the auctioneer, the man next to him whispered, "He's a real haggler. Drives a hard bargain. But I don't think he'll get much for this next servant—she looks too young to be an experienced worker."

Servant? Ricky didn't have a clue what the man was talking about. Then he looked at the stage and saw Mia standing near the auctioneer. Mia's contract was up for sale! She looked horrified. "Trade the Trader," Ricky whispered to himself, as he remembered the game's instructions.

"Now here is a brand new girl," said the auctioneer. "No experience, BUT think of the training possibilities!" Mia looked outraged—the thought of being sold as a servant was unbearable.

Ricky walked toward the auctioneer. "I'll give you twenty pieces of gold for her," he said. Mia glared at him.

The auctioneer smiled a wry smile. "My good man, she is worth at least four times that."

Ricky screwed up his nose and shook his head. "She's untrained. I'll have to start from scratch. She could prove to be very difficult."

"Fifty pieces," said the auctioneer. "Still a bargain by anyone's standards."

"More like a small fortune for someone who could prove worthless." Ricky laughed as Mia went red. He'd pay for that comment later. "I tell you what, how about thirty-five?"

"Forty-five," replied the auctioneer curtly.

Ricky turned and pretended he had lost interest.

"Forty!" yelled the auctioneer.

"Done!" said Ricky with a smile.

"You drive a hard bargain, young man," said the auctioneer. "I don't recognize you, so I want immediate payment. I no longer accept gems or goods. Too many crooks around these days."

It was then Ricky remembered that he didn't actually have any gold. He felt in his pockets. All he had was half a bus ticket and a piece of chewing gum.

"Problem?" asked the auctioneer.

"Ahhh, I seem to have forgotten my money pouch," said Ricky sheepishly.

"Oh, well," sighed the auctioneer, "looks like this servant's contract is back up for sale."

"Wait!" cried Mia, looking desperately at Ricky. "Give him your watch as payment."

"What!" said Ricky. "But I love this watch! It's waterproof and has a message sender, a calculator, and a stopwatch."

"What about ME?" yelled Mia, as the auctioneer put up the For Sale sign again.

"Chill out," said Ricky, handing over his watch. "Here, take my watch for the girl." The auctioneer gingerly fingered the watch. He had never seen anything like it.

Suddenly a man came running through the crowd toward them, screaming, "That's a witch's cat!" He was chasing Curiosity.

Curiosity jumped into Ricky's arms for safety. Ricky leaped up onto the stage with Mia. Everyone in the market was staring at them suspiciously.

Spotting Fortune's wheel on the auctioneer's table, Mia grabbed it. "Time to get out of here!" she yelled as she spun the arrow.

"Green," cried Ricky. "Hang on! That's the Raider!"

They were spinning out of the marketplace and out of control!

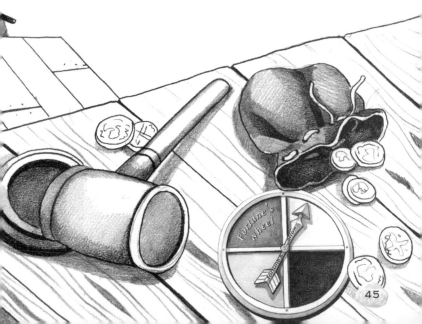

CHAPTER 6

Raid the Raider

"Ouch!" yelped Ricky, peeling Curiosity off his head. "Watch your claws, you dumb cat. Let go! Mia, move your elbow—it's breaking my ribs." Mia struggled to her feet. They had landed in some bushes, on a dune behind a beach.

"How could you!" cried Mia angrily, through clenched teeth.

"What?" asked Ricky, untangling himself from a bush.

"You hesitated swapping your watch, for ME! Your best friend!" She looked at her wrist, pretending to look at a watch, and imitated Ricky. "But it's waterproof, with a message sender and whatever else! . . . And what did you mean—could prove worthless?"

"I was playing the game," said Ricky getting to his feet. "You know—bargaining before you trade. I couldn't really tell him you're worth a million dollars, could I? Come on, Mia. You know I was joking."

Just then, they heard voices coming from the beach. They crawled to the top of the dune and peered over it.

"Pirates," whispered Ricky. A ship was anchored
in the bay. Five men and the pirate captain
surrounded an open chest on the beach. One of
the men was on his knees. His head was bowed,
and his hands were bound behind his back. The
other men stood over him.

"Come on, Captain," said one of the pirates,
pointing at the kneeling man. "Let me take care
of him." He drew his sword.

The captain shook his head. "Not until he tells us what happened to my treasure." He turned to the man. "Aye! I'd speak quick if I was you. They don't call me the meanest, black-hearted pirate of the seven seas for nothing." He put his hand on his sword and leaned closer. "I'll make it less painful for you if you come clean and tell me, Crazy Campbell."

Curiosity hissed and jumped when she heard that name.

"Oh, no!" Mia gasped. "Did you hear that, Ricky? They're going to kill Crazy Campbell."

"Shh," said Ricky. "He looks like he's about to say something."

They could see Crazy Campbell shaking. "I . . . I told you before, Captain, I . . . I don't know where your treasure is."

"Well, what were you doing snooping around my treasure chest when my crew found you, hey?" snarled the captain.

"I was looking for a way out of here. It's like I already told you. I was looking for a thing called Fortune's wheel. You see, I hesitated and now it seems like I'm trapped forever. I thought maybe the wheel was in the treasure chest. But I never took any of your treasure. The chest was empty when I found it."

"I don't want to hear any more stories," yelled the captain. "If you can't tell me where my treasure is, you're no use to me." He drew his sword. At that same moment, Mia leaped out of hiding and onto the beach.

"NO!" she screamed, grabbing two swords from the unsuspecting pirates. She threw one to Ricky. "Block them, Ricky!" she cried, sawing at Crazy Campbell's ropes.

The pirates had been stunned at first, but they now began to circle Mia, Ricky, and Crazy Campbell. The captain gave a mean grin. "So you're the ones who have my treasure, eh?" He threatened, "I'll give you one chance to come clean."

Mia's heart was racing. They couldn't win a sword fight, so what could they do? As Ricky shuffled around, his foot hit something in the sand. He tripped and staggered backward.

"Aha!" said one of the pirates, shoving Ricky. "You're not so brave now! I think your luck has run out."

Bracing himself for a blow, Ricky looked down to see what had tripped him. It was Fortune's wheel! He grabbed it and spun the arrow. It landed on the color blue. "Crusader!" he cried, and once again, everything began to wildly spin around and around.

CHAPTER 7

Meeting the Invader

Thud! They landed on the ground in front of a huge, wooden door.

"That was close," panted Mia, helping Ricky to his feet. "Good one, Ricky. Talk about lucky."

"I'll say," said Crazy Campbell, feeling his wrists. His voice surprised them because they hadn't realized someone else could join their game. Curiosity hissed and clawed at his leg.

"I don't think she likes you," said Ricky. "Every time someone mentions your name, she has that same reaction."

"Mrs. Oxley's cat, right?" he said, staring at Curiosity. "This cat had a little trouble with one of my dogs when she was a kitten. She'll be all right once she's told me what she thinks." Sure enough, after what could only be described as a hissy fit, Curiosity calmed down. She even let Crazy Campbell pat her.

"She probably feels a lot better now," laughed Crazy Campbell. "Having something on your mind for too long can really weigh you down."

"Something like looking for treasure?" asked Ricky cautiously. He wanted to see if Crazy Campbell really was as mad as Mrs. Oxley said.

Crazy Campbell shook his head and gave a hearty laugh. "I suppose looking for treasure drove me a little nutty at times, but I'm not crazy. Sometimes people call you names because they just don't understand what you're doing. I don't mind the name, though. I think it gives me character." Crazy Campbell held his arm and grimaced with pain.

Mia noticed a gash in his arm. "Did the pirates do that?" she asked.

Crazy Campbell shook his head. "No, not the pirates. I got this when I Invaded the Invaders." He saw the shocked looks on their faces. "You haven't been there, have you? That's where I became stuck in this awful game."

"How did you do that?" asked Ricky.

"Well, I just ran in there, knocked that invader king right off his throne, and seized the crown. It wasn't really that hard. Then I gave a huge party to celebrate my new title. It was an enormous feast—very grand. Food, song, dance. No expense was spared!" He grinned.

"No, no! We mean, how did you get stuck in the game?" asked Mia.

"Oh!" Crazy Campbell's smile faded. "When I spotted Fortune's wheel, I wasn't ready to stop being king because I was having such a great time. So, I put the wheel in the pocket of my robe and thought I'd spin it later. I let all that good fortune go to my head." He gave a bitter laugh. "Anyway, while I was sleeping, the real king came back with a huge army and took back his title and crown. I woke up in the dungeon—a prisoner! The good days were over."

"How come you didn't just spin the wheel and move on?" asked Ricky.

"I tried, but it wouldn't work anymore. Then I remembered what the instructions said:

Miss me once, and the treasure is lost.
Only then will you know the true cost."

"What does that mean?" asked Ricky.

"It means," sighed Crazy Campbell heavily, "that if you miss your opportunity, you lose one of the most precious things you have—your freedom. So I became trapped in the game. When you two started to play, my Fortune's wheel started to work again. I spotted you at the market. Curiosity caused quite a stir, didn't she?" Crazy Campbell bent down and stroked her on her back.

"And then we found you at the beach," said Ricky. "But we didn't have time to Raid the Raiders. So why did the wheel appear again?"

Crazy Campbell grinned mischievously.

"You *did* steal their treasure!" cried Mia.

"I didn't exactly steal it!" said Crazy. "I just put it somewhere else. They'll find it eventually." He got up. "Now, where are we? Crusader, wasn't it? We'd better hurry up and start the next task. I don't want to get on fortune's bad side again!"

"Wait a minute," said Mia, looking a little pale. "Does this mean that if we fail this task, we're trapped in the game, too?"

"That seems to be the way the game works," said Crazy Campbell flatly. "At least I invaded the Invader for you, so there's only one place left to go! We might be lucky."

Ricky and Mia exchanged worried looks.

CHAPTER 8

Crusade Mountain

Ricky, Mia, and Crazy Campbell put their weight against the huge door. It moved slowly. Their mouths fell open. In front of them was a mountain of treasure. There were overflowing cauldrons of brightly colored gems and chests of gold and silver bars. Golden chains, priceless plates and cups, jugs of pearls, statues, and paintings were all piled high.

"The vault of the Knights Templar," whispered Crazy Campbell.

Mia and Ricky remained still. This was the most spectacular thing they had ever seen.

A message was painted on the floor, at the base of the mountain of treasure. Mia read it aloud.

Climb the mountain and start your crusade. You will find your treasure at its peak. It holds the thing you most seek!

"Sounds easy enough," said Ricky. "I wonder what the catch is."

"Let's start climbing and find out," said Crazy Campbell, putting his foot on the nearest chest.

They climbed slowly. It seemed surprisingly easy. At the halfway mark, however, the mountain started to tremble. It soon became harder and harder to keep their footing. Chests, pots, and cauldrons rolled loose, and treasure started to slide down the mountain. They were ducking flying gems, statues, and gold and silver bars.

"Look out!" cried Mia as a huge bucket of rubies toppled down.

A noise from below sounded ominous. The floor of the vault started to split, and they looked down into a deep, black hole.

"Hold on tight!" yelled Crazy. "We don't want to fall into that!"

They climbed cautiously, only taking hold of the most solid chests. Dragging himself up, Ricky could see the peak of the mountain. One small chest was perched right at the top. "We're almost there!" he gasped.

Curiosity reached it first—then Ricky. "It won't open!" he said, struggling with the lock. Mia reached the chest and read the message on its lid:

Six heads in a dead man's chest.
Two more and the curse can rest.

"Oh, no! It's the curse!" she cried.

Crazy Campbell looked gravely at the message. The mountain was now shaking violently, so they clasped hands. "Don't look down," cried Crazy. "Hold on."

The roof of the vault cracked, and a streak of light shone through the narrow slit.

"Ricky! Mia!" yelled a voice. It was Uncle Earl!

"Help! We're trapped!" they pleaded. "It's the curse . . ."

"Listen carefully!" screamed Uncle Earl over the noise of crashing treasure. "I'm going to send something down through the opening. Put it in the chest. Don't lose it. It may be your only chance."

"Hurry!" yelled Ricky. "I don't think the mountain's going to hold much longer."

Uncle Earl lowered a small bundle tied to a piece of rope through the slit. Ricky reached out and grabbed it.

"I've got it!" said Ricky. Mia held the chest while Crazy Campbell hit the lock with a gold bar. Finally, the lock snapped. Ricky untied the bundle to find the double-headed coin. As he passed the coin to Mia, the mountain seemed to heave, and the coin fell into a cauldron near the floor of the vault.

"Oh, no! We've lost it!" he yelled.

Curiosity leaped down the shaking mountain, scratching and hissing as jewels hit her. She reached the cauldron, and her head disappeared. They held their breath. She emerged with the coin between her teeth and carefully made her way back. With a final leap, she dropped the coin into the chest.

Gradually the shaking subsided. Ricky and Mia hugged each other, and Crazy Campbell laughed. But their relief was short-lived. The vault began to fill with water.

"Grab the rope!" yelled Uncle Earl. "Quickly! Climb as fast as you can."

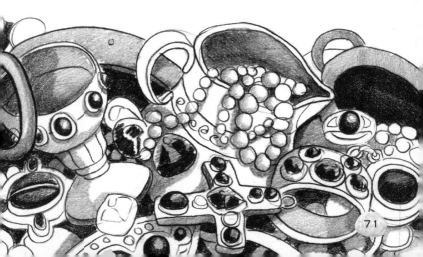

CHAPTER 9

Real Treasure

Ricky was the last one out of the hole. As Uncle Earl helped him, Ricky felt cold water lapping at his feet. Looking down, they watched as the vault crumbled in on itself.

"Everyone OK?" asked Uncle Earl, giving Mia and Ricky a big hug. Curiosity purred and licked her paws. The early morning sun felt wonderful. They took deep breaths. It was good to be free of the game.

"You saved us just in time," said Mia. "But how did you know we were down there?"

"I didn't," said Uncle Earl smiling. "I wanted to show you the coin that Mrs. Oxley had found. It's called a dead man's coin. This kind of coin used to be given to people as a warning. I thought it might have something to do with the curse. Anyway, when I couldn't find you, I guessed that you must have rowed over to Oak Island. Sure enough, when I got here, I found Mrs. Oxley's boat."

Uncle Earl looked at Mia and Ricky. "I knew you two would be involved somehow. Then I heard screaming, and suddenly the earth began to split open! I heard Mia reading the curse, so I tied up the coin, and you know the rest."

"We're so glad you did!" said Mia.

"That's for sure!" laughed Crazy Campbell.

Uncle Earl said, "You are a dirty, ragged lot. So what's in that tumbling mountain of treasure?"

Ricky, Mia, and Crazy Campbell glanced at each other. Should they tell Uncle Earl about the game? Curiosity hissed and meowed.

"Well, it must be good," said Uncle Earl.

"Oh, it's good all right. But I've had my last spin at finding the treasure. I'm retiring from this game," said Crazy Campbell.

"We'll tell you all about it later, Uncle Earl. Promise," said Mia, with a huge smile.

"Yeah," agreed Ricky, stretching as he took more deep breaths of fresh air. "Right now, Uncle Earl, getting out of there is the best treasure of all!"

The Real
OAK ISLAND

Oak Island is a small island off the coast of Nova Scotia, Canada. Legend says that treasure is buried in a pit on the island. In 1795, a teenager named Daniel McGinnis uncovered what he believed to be a site for buried treasure. With the help of friends, he began to dig. As they went deeper, a series of wooden log platforms blocked the hole. They gave up digging, but returned years later to continue the hunt. They were forced to abandon their search, however, because the hole kept filling with water.

Over the next 200 years, people tried to find what was hidden in the hole. So much time and effort have been spent on the search for treasure that the site has become known as the Money Pit. The things found so far—gold chains, coins, parchment, a stone with strange writing—are thought to be clues to the treasure.

The peculiar writing on the stone supposedly has been translated as saying treasure is buried forty feet below.

There are many different theories as to who may have buried the treasure on Oak Island. Some believe it may have been buried by pirates, possibly the famous pirate Captain Kidd. Other people think it could have been buried by a group called the Knights Templar.

What is at the bottom of the pit remains a mystery to this day. And you never know—there may be no treasure at all!

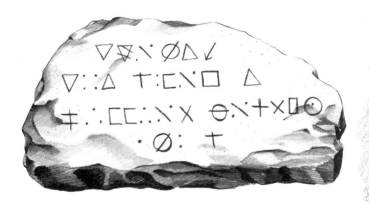

Glossary

archaeology studying the past by digging up buildings and objects

cauldron a large, round metal pot

causeway a raised path across low or wet ground

curiosity wanting to know about many things

curtly rudely; briefly

escapade a wild adventure

gingerly moving cautiously

grimaced made a facial expression showing pain

haggler someone who is good at bargaining

hissy fit a hissing display of disapproval

hoarder someone who stores things away for another day

immense very large

indentured servant bound to work for another for a given amount of time

inscribed something carved on an object

lapping water washing or beating against the shore

meager lacking in necessities

shuffled moved and dragged feet along the ground

snarled spoke in a fierce and angry way

surveillance a close watch kept over an area by police or security people

theories ideas to explain something

trespassers those who enter a property without permission

vault a strong room where valuables are kept

wry slightly amused

Titles in This Series

Quest for the Cup

On the Trail of the Golden Man

In Search of the Egyptian Queen

Digging for Buried Treasure

Diving for the Ghost Galleon

Racing for the Birdman

Decoding the Mayan Marvels

Saving Atlantis